Yes, Let's

Johns Hopkins: Poetry and Fiction
John T. Irwin, General Editor

POETRY TITLES IN THE SERIES

John Hollander, *"Blue Wine" and Other Poems*
Robert Pack, *Waking to My Name: New and Selected Poems*
Philip Dacey, *The Boy under the Bed*
Wyatt Prunty, *The Times Between*
Barry Spacks, *Spacks Street: New and Selected Poems*
Gibbons Ruark, *Keeping Company*
David St. John, *Hush*
Wyatt Prunty, *What Women Know, What Men Believe*
Adrien Stoutenberg, *Land of Superior Mirages: New and Selected Poems*
John Hollander, *In Time and Place*
Charles Martin, *Steal the Bacon*
John Bricuth, *The Heisenberg Variations*
Tom Disch, *Yes, Let's: New and Selected Poems*

Tom Disch

Yes, Let's

New and Selected Poems

THE JOHNS HOPKINS UNIVERSITY PRESS
BALTIMORE AND LONDON

This book has been brought to publication with the generous assistance of the G. Harry Pouder Fund and the Albert Dowling Trust.

The Johns Hopkins University Press
701 West 40th Street, Baltimore, Maryland 21211
The Johns Hopkins Press Ltd., London

The paper used in this publication meets the minimum requirements of American National Standard for Information Sciences—Permanence of Paper for Printed Library Materials, ANSI Z39.48–1984.

LIBRARY OF CONGRESS CATALOGING-IN-PUBLICATION DATA

Disch, Thomas M.
  Yes, let's.
  (Johns Hopkins, poetry and fiction)
PS3554.I8Y4   1989   811'.54   88–46116
ISBN 0–8018–3835–5
ISBN 0–8010–3851–7 (pbk.)

Previously published poems appeared in the following volumes or in the periodicals listed below.

The Right Way to Figure Plumbing, © 1972 Thomas M. Disch (Basilisk Press); *ABCDEFG HIJKLM NPOQRST UVWXYZ*, © 1981 Thomas M. Disch (Hutchinson); *Burn This*, © 1982 Thomas M. Disch (Hutchinson); *Orders of the Retina*, © 1982 Thomas M. Disch (Toothpaste Press); *Here I Am, There You Are, Where Were We*, © 1984 Thomas M. Disch (Hutchinson).

Amazing Stories: "Skydiver"; *Boulevard:* "March"; *City:* "Slides"; *Epoch:* "A Cow of Our Time"; *Lake Street Review:* "Tale of the Forebears"; *New Republic:* "Dreams: A Darwinian View"; *Paris Review:* "MCMLXXXIV"; *Poetry:* "The Argument Resumed," "The Viewers and the Viewed: Eurailpass Verses, 1985," "In Defense of Forest Lawn," "Working on a Tan," "Entropic Villanelle"; *Shenandoah:* "Symbols of Love and Death," "At the Grave of Amy Clampitt"; and *Times Literary Supplement:* "Short Flight," "Swimming." "Birth of a Pillow" first appeared as a Bellevue Press broadside.

for Charles Naylor

Contents

Acknowledgments   xiii

New Poems *(1988)*
The Argument Resumed; or, Up through Tribeca   3
Short Flight   4
MCMLXXXIV   5
Skydiver   11
Dreams: A Darwinian View   12
Symbols of Love and Death   13
At the Grave of Amy Clampitt   14
The Viewers and the Viewed: Eurailpass Verses, 1985   15
Slides   17
In Defense of Forest Lawn   18
Sin and Punishment   20
Birth of a Pillow   21
Tales of the Forebears   23
Working on a Tan   24
Swimming   27
Entropic Villanelle   29
March   30
A Cow of Our Time   31

From **The Right Way to Figure Plumbing** *(1972)*
To Jean-Ann   35
The Blindman's Sign   36
My Mother: A Discussion   37
Everything Closes after Midnight: A London Lament   38
Convalescing in London   39
"The Surprise"   40

Portrait of a Tourist   41
A Vacation on Earth   42
Learning to Cross the Street   43

From **ABCDEFG HIJKLM NPOQRST UVWXYZ** *(1981)*
Abecedary   47
An Allegory   49
The Art of Dying   50
At the Tomb of the Unknown President   51
The Color Blue   52
The Doppelgänger   53
D. W. Richmond Gives Directions to the Architect of
    His Tomb   54
Eternity   55
Homage to the Carracci   56
How to Behave when Dead   57
May   58
A Note to Romeo   59
Questions Your Children Are Certain to Ask   60
The Rapist's Villanelle   61
Zewhyexary   62

From **Burn This** *(1982)*
High Purpose in Poetry: A Primer   67
For Marilyn Hacker   70
Praise   71
Poems   73
A Concise History of Music   74
A Bookmark   75

From **Orders of the Retina** *(1982)*

The Goldberg Variations   79

Litany   80

The Childhood of Language   81

What It Was Like   82

Turner Jigsaw   83

The Prisoners of War   84

Coming of Age   85

What to Accept   86

From **Here I Am, There You Are, Where Were We** *(1984)*

Here I Am

Coal Miners   89

Prayer to Pleasure   91

Just before the Cops Arrive   93

Waking in a Strange Apartment   95

There You Are

Ode on the Source of the Clitumnus   97

Ode on the Source of the Foux   99

For a Derelict   101

You Can Own This Painting for $75   102

When Your Hand Shakes, when Your Eye's Meat   104

When Your Eyes Meet, when Your Hand Shakes   105

Where Were We

A Catalogue   107

Alcohol Island: A Chronicle   108

The Clouds   109

Yes, Let's   112

Acknowledgments

Necessarily, this book of poems is dedicated to Charles Naylor, who has been, since 1969, its enabling presence and the *You* my *I* has most steadily had in mind.

Many others aided and abetted, and I'd like to acknowledge those debts as well: John Irwin, who suggested a *New and Selected Poems* before I'd had the temerity. Richard Howard, who in my fledgling days amazed me with a nod and a smile. Marilyn Hacker, David Lehman, and Dana Gioia, for steady infusions of camaraderie and criticism. David Lunde, Peter Jay, and Alan Kornblum, for publishing three of the books from which these poems were selected, and a host of magazine editors whose pages supplied the frames for these various pictures. As this incomplete list suggests, poetry is not a lonely pursuit.

New Poems

(1988)

The Argument Resumed;
or, Up through Tribeca

It may not be forever, but
The zing of beauty in the middle
Of the day—this little kid, for instance,
Heading home in his stroller,
Radiantly silly in a knitted snowsuit,
Or those windows of snazzy bowls
A few blocks back, all of solid wood
But gleaming as from a kiln
(Somebody should pay good money for that.
Ah, to be rich!). . . . The zing, I say,
An dich as we take our constitutional
Does add a luster when a luster is needed,
And if that luster fades as we proceed
Elsewhere, there's no call to be
Bereft. We are left with our store
Of memories: the scent, maybe, of a herbal rinse
Familiar from childhood. Or the sky may echo
The blue of a favorite tie. But "forever"?
Doesn't that tend to detract from the glory
Of the thing? Glory must burst
On us like fireworks. If the gleam
Or the sweetness isn't fleeting,
How shall it bear repeating?
How should we dare to eat another
Sundae of sunsets? See where a peach
Glows among other peaches in the fruitbowl.
Such and no other is the soul.

Short Flight

As our hypothetical flight continues and the sunset's
Lovely slide show begins its introduction
To the lecture of night, we can glimpse through the scrim
Of lingerie-colored clouds the patterns of the utopia
We are leaving: the looms of a million Penelopes,
The lawns, the jeweled pawnshops, lotus pools
And libraries—all the emblematic paraphernalia of our consensus
Shrunk to the dimensions of a sheet of foolscap.
Then, whack, the window must be shuttered,
For the flight attendant has announced the evening's dream,
Which will be one we've already seen, years ago,
On TV; but never mind, it's free, and there is complimentary wine
To ease our transition to where, amazingly,
We have already arrived, home to the movies and our lives.

MCMLXXXIV

M

Two sharp eminences with a valley between
Through which the erratic witness of a loosened tongue
Flows to the sea: Mount M———. Mark it well.
It is the same mystifying letter that masks
My middle name. At confirmation that became
Mark, but neither name nor sacrament stuck,
And I was tumbled into a universe
In which that M could stand for almost anything,
Into the infamous Modern World where meanings
Are all relative and relatives don't mean as much
As they did in A.D. 1000 in the Mediterranean basin
Where our earlier world-view was formed by conniving
Clerics (cf. Jack Goody, *The Development of the Family*
And Marriage in Europe), but that's not to say
They don't mean a lot or we wouldn't be traveling
Thousands of miles to visit them, would we?
The engine hums, the road swerves, and the valley
Opens to a view of the Pacific. Wow. One sees at once
Why science believes the moon to have been
Scooped from its basin, for it is huge. Meanwhile,
High above our tiny Dodge (named for Aries, alias
The Ram), the angel of my middle name
Sings of sunlight, sea and shore, praises
The magma at earth's core, swings his censer,
Scents the air and shouts, Behold, am I not fair!

C

In the universe determined by the letter
C, the ocean seems invisible behind its security
Blanket of fog, as absconding as those gods we've chosen
Lately to disbelieve in, though the creeds
They taught us can still be professed at moments
Of uncertainty or stress. A hundred
Curious events happen here that happen nowhere
Else, coincidences too odd to credit
Except that we have seen them with our eyes:
Ice palaces created by the condensed December
Breath of sleeping bees; a replica in sugar cubes
Of Bernini's imposing colonnade; a great aluminum C
In Civil Rights Square formed from a hundred
Million crushed Pepsi cans commemorating Michelson
And Morley's epoch-making experiment of 1887 that proves
That everything moves at the same speed if viewed
From the right angle. Nor is that all there is to see,
For look up there at the peak some people call
The Crest of Charlemagne and others simply
Charlie's Nose. Lesser letters—an H, a D, an N,
Even the eager-beaver vowels—can't really compare.
O might be thought more all-encompassing
But it excludes too much, achieves closure
Too easily; it could never become, as C so often does,
A cradle or a caudle bowl. X is more versatile,
Will stand, quite literally, for any value you give it,
But you can't cuddle up to an X. U is the closest
Any letter comes to C, and it's certainly true
That I love U, but only because I learned to love
C first. C, this is for you. Love, T.

M

My, my, there it is again, the hum
Of the millennium—*Om, Om*—the tom-tom mantra
Of a mind that has become all mouth,
Hermetically sealed against sense
And immense with its own malarky:
Me, now, or Emma Bovary in a moment
Of immortal longing. Such a thin line
Separates madness from mediocrity,
Manna from mania, the lover's sigh *M'ama!*
And babyhood's redoubled cry *Mama, Mama!*
Is it then only Echo who answers Amen?
Is man to be blamed for insensate greed
If the maw to be filled was willed from time
Immemorial by the great I Am That I Am?
No one blames Him for His huge needs.
Place a microscopic microphone among
The thousand flowers where a millipede
Brunches and you will hear the same murmur
Of hunger appeased. *Mm,* purrs the millipede,
Mm-good. No doubt it is without nobility
Thus to yield to the messes we crave,
But did not the Lord who made the iamb
Make it to lie down with the yam?

L

How well, our anchormen ask us when news is scarce,
Or how poorly did Orwell score prophetically?
Is there fear in truth? Has anyone been bought and sold
This year we didn't usually buy and sell before?
What knell does curfew toll? Who put poor Pussy
In the well? How now do we spell Mao? Will Shell
Be swallowed whole by Exxon? Can we mend the crack
In Ma Bell's back? How long can we count on
Iran and Iraq to keep on the attack, and could other
Lesser breeds be trained at the same good work? Last
But not least, what rough beast, or rather what sorrow
Has Frank got in store for us tomorrow? Will there be
Mirth in Mudville or hell on earth? Will angels weep
An acid rain to see that man has lived in vain?
Will generals tire of their games, washing the poems
Of Sandinist rebels from their beaches? Will the tide turn?
Will the fire burn? And whom? Will empire gel in time
For the summer Olympics? *Quien sabe?* as our friends
Across the border say, and now here's Jane to explain
What that means and to tell us something old,
Something new, something borrowed, and something blue
About Ella Fitzgerald. Jane? We seem to be
Experiencing some technical difficulties, but please
Bear with us. We'll be back after this message.

XXX

Like as the wave makes toward the pebbled shore
And kisses it, so does her lustful customer kiss
The blistered whore, heedless of the risk of herpes,
Temporarily insane and then, after the sweetness
Of yielding, possessed by an equal giddiness
Retreating. So too the wave retires down the beach,
Rearranging all those pebbles, but then, as though
Not satisfied with that arrangement, returning
To kiss them again. So might a miser kiss
The gold doubloons and louis d'or spread like butter
On the English muffin of her bed. Then, as that miser
(Think of Zazu Pitts in her final scenes in *Greed*)
Must restore her treasures to their trove, so does the sea
Rescind its outreachings, only upon consideration
To resume its kisses, as lovers do, unwearying, or
Even if wearying, renewing them anyhow the way that
Landlords must renew their tenants' leases, whether
They will or no, being compelled by laws they did not make
And cannot break, though they may (as ours has once again)
Take them back temporarily. The leases, that is, not the laws
Or the kisses, which are, as bottles once, non-returnable,
And which still along this pebbled shore accrue
Like interest to an IRA account compounded daily
In some microchip, its own small sea of data surging
In bits and bytes and Microsoft _{TM} electric kisses
Of X and O, yes and no, stop and go, high tide
And low—which, as the moon is full, will come tonight at six,
When I in my high rubber boots with my little plastic bucket
Will once again be out on the beach, a sea-maddened
Tourist hunting for agates in the shingle, fleeing
The ocean's kiss and feeling, as I flee, its tingle.

IV

Slowly the level of the fluid climbs
Up through the branching plastic vines
Of library and club, inexorable as genealogy,
To where the brokers of power are sprawled
In leather wingback chairs. Beware, sirs,
O beware! Blue veins pulse in drooping hands.
A finger twitches and begins to itch, as the vines
Wreathe round oak legs and writhe up these half-alive
Forms, writhe up and twist in lissome nooses round
Limp wrists, flabby forearms, slumped shoulders,
To press at last against the carotids and plunge
The business-suited world in sleep. A hush
Falls o'er the quad. The widest eye, the best-laid brick
Cannot resist the balm of a long-predicted
Year-by-year-delayed demise. It comes,
Their demi-death, as no surprise, but as a kind
Of relaxation. Some mortar crumbles by
A caryatid's toe; a liveried attendant
Hears the members snore and quietly removes
Cups and journals from their liver-spotted fingertips.
Can this be the end of the line? Can this be 1984?

Skydiver

Hurled from the hatch of a rational life,
He hurtles through the blue above us,
Borne up by the model democracy of molecules
Bumping into each other at random, and though
That may sound snide or flip, it's just my way
Of talking: I honestly feel amazement, only that,
At Man, the mighty copycat, who just by looking
At a dandelion has come up—and now floats
Down—with this, the supreme expression
Of faith in things unseen: the wind,
The mind, the patient skill of seamstresses
Running immense lengths of nylon
Through their clamoring machines.

Dreams: A Darwinian View

Before December had been named,
Or wolves or fire been well tamed,
When Man was but a shivering ape
Caught by the glaciers with no escape,
The snowbound nights, and days, as well,
Were a veritable hell,
And of the trials he had to bear
The worst were time and dread and care.
He could not simply hibernate:
Each dawn he had to wake, and wait
Through all the hours of a day
That wishing could not wish away—
And so he dreamt, and in his dreams
Abolished *is,* invented *seems.*
He passed the time, and time passed by,
And so may you, and so shall I.

Symbols of Love and Death

The whole room smells of rust
because the steam came on today

The only letter in the mailbox
was from some nowhere poet
who got drunk with me three years ago
He needs five hundred dollars
for his legal defense

On the sunbathing terrace of my gym
a clotheslinefull of Chinese lanterns
jiggles in the winter wind

The margins of my Bantam
Ovid crumble when I make notes

                    There is
a particular sad way someone may smile
when love is suddenly served up to her
The billows rising as the silver bell
is lifted from the plate

Or how she hurries from the restaurant
slamming doors, no longer human
a piece of paper
blowing down the street

At the Grave of Amy Clampitt

All of Nature's noblest metonymies have come
As our mutes to mourn with us here on her behalf:
The inconsolable clouds, the ominous cut flowers,
The grass with its grim reminder of the large
Lawnmower Fate drives o'er the plots
Of all our little lives. *Hélas!* But even so,
How lovely. The pebblings of the granite
Are the shingle on Eternity's stillest beach,
And see there, with the raindrops filling it
And spilling from the letters' discreet serifs—
Her name incised in the immotive sand,
Nothing exotic or very grand but eminently
Suitable to her new estate: she is a monument
At last among the multitude that she has visited
To lay her wreaths, bequeath her song, and get
A piece of the inaction that passesth all understanding.

The Viewers and the Viewed:
Eurailpass Verses, 1985

1. SCENES OF COMMON LIFE

Amsterdam

With drunken smiles and apple cheeks,
In wide-brimmed hats and ruffs bleached white,
The ancient burghers all concur:
Be rich and of good appetite!—
Advice that these museum-goers
Attend with faces carved from granite,
As though these old Dutch businessmen
Were creatures from another planet
And not the patterns upon which
Their genes were fashioned stitch by stitch.

2. AMONG THE EARLIER GERMAN PAINTERS

Hanover and Munich

Brute rage and cruelty have here full rein,
Where Christs are pierced and whipped and steeped in pain
And endless holy martyrs feel the thrust
Of voyeurism's disembodied lust.
Such (we later viewers apprehend)
Is every felon's destined end
Who raises challenge to the Church or State,
And *would* have been Herr Martin Luther's fate:
A hint that many of today's Bavarians
So heeded they became themselves barbarians
In zesty, zealous imitation of
The blows and bludgeons of the Lord God's love
And now, as henchmen, share immortal blame
For what the German Church and State became.

3. SAAL X

Vienna

Two lions menace us just halfway up
The stairs, where Theseus prepares to club
A centaur: we're entering the realm
Of art and must beware. Here even apples
In the hands of Flemish Eves may pose a threat,
And hell spawns demons right and left. There's worse
To come, and yet with what a cool aplomb
The noble rich who share these rooms look on,
Their eyes fast fixed upon their portraitists.

The worst atrocities are in Saal X:
No Spanish martyrdoms, no flayed Marsyas,
No writhings of the buxom damned, but life
As Pieter Breughel saw it, calm as any
Prince hung on these walls, and not without a sense
Of fun. He'd have enjoyed the constant zaps
Of buzzers triggered by the mesmerized
Museum visitors as they trespass
Beyond the boundaries set by velvet ropes
To grimace at his grim particulars.

Slides

This is a shot I took
of Charles and Marilyn
and the Grand Canyon.
The building over on the right, just inside
the picture, is where we ate
that night, I think.

This is the Grand Canyon,

and this is another view.

Me,

Charles again,

and here's Marilyn in the swimsuit
she found in Missouri.
This must be out of place.

Ah, here it is
at sunset.
Some of them didn't come out
the way we hoped,
but they give you an idea.

The cabin we stayed in.
Look at the dust on that car!

Marilyn and me.

Charles and Marilyn

Me and Charles
with the sign at the exit behind us.

And this is the last one.
They say it's a mile deep.

In Defense of Forest Lawn

In his poem "Tract" William Carlos Williams
recommends a style for funerals
much like the style he practiced
as a poet: a "rough plain hearse"
resembling a farm wagon, its driver
demoted to walk alongside holding the reins,
and the mourners riding after
with conspicuous inconvenience, open
"to the weather as to grief."

In horse-and-buggy days, perhaps,
such a scenario might have worked,
but nowadays much-weathered wood denotes
deluxe accommodations. A triumph
for Williams' esthetics, but the problem
remains: how to bury people simply
and tastefully, without on the one hand
holding up traffic unduly or on the other
treating the corpse like industrial waste.

Personally I think that Forest Lawn
has got just about the right combination
of hokum and expedience, gravitas and pizazz.
People are inclined to laugh at Forest Lawn,
having been instructed by Evelyn Waugh
that only the Sovereign Pontiff can *own*
the Pietà, that Europe has the copyright
on class, and that Americans had better stick
to. . . . What would he suggest: farm wagons?

But if Romans did well to copy Greek originals,
if museums needn't be embarrassed by their casts—
if, that is, form and not seignoralty
is our ideal, then why shouldn't Forest Lawn
heap as much of the enmarbled past
on the plates of our grief as, say,
Westminster Abbey or St. Paul's? Why shouldn't
the dead, God damn it, be allowed one Parthian
shot at greatness? Aren't wakes for feasting?

Suppose we did it in the minimalist way
Williams suggests, bankrupting florists
and stonecutters. Do you think the heirs
in their enhanced prosperity would endow
posterity with anything so grand or lush
as a properly got-up cemetery? Think again.
How, I wonder, did Waugh himself get planted?
Opulently, I'm sure. So, gentlemen, if you'll step
Over here, I'd like to show you our brochure.

Sin and Punishment

For sins of obesity I am caught
In the trap of my boot, whose laces
Elude my waggling fingertips,
Whose tongue will not cease
Telling my weight and fortune
Until I have performed a ritual
Humbling of head to foot.

For sins of biliousness I wear
This belt and collar. See,
By my changed complexion, how
This double ring of levees saves
My head with its deep furrows
Of purpose and confusion
From the blood's flash floods.

For sins of false economy I fly,
As from a mast, this length of silk,
Whose broad diagonals convey
In long since broken codes
The price I may be hired at
To wear the colors of my class
And, too, the price I'm willing to pay you.

For sins of inattentiveness my eyes
Perpetually are made to kiss
These plastic discs by whose
Incessant action I may see, within
The shop windows of common agreement,
The frilly underwear of our beloved
Empress, Earth.

Birth of a Pillow

Each day—*almost* each day—as though I were
Walking in a circle, I find myself passing
        This place again—
And here I am again, and here it is,
For that is the nature of a monument,
        To be where simply
As a citizen you must pass by
And tip your hat and say "Hello again"
        And smile to think
The useless thing's immutable, as churches
Seem to be once they are built, or bridges,
        Or the grander sort
Of store. Who could, for instance, credit Gimbel's
Closing down? Or Bloomingdale's? And yet
        I worked at Klein's
Some twenty years ago, and now there's nothing
But a barbershop that keeps the whole damned block
        From being wrecked.
Odd, to be grateful such a hulk endures.
Back in my stockboy days, a Cooper Union
        Dropout dreaming
I'd become (if not a prince) an architect,
I would have gladly let the wrecking balls
        Knock down one half
Of Manhattan, starting with Klein's. Clothing, too,
Becomes precious simply by having lasted.
        I'm wholly unable
To throw away my old blue-green sports coat
(From Brooks Brothers) though it is years too small.
        But here's a thought:
What if I made a pillow of it, preserving
The breast pocket and a buttonhole or two,
        As architects
Preserve the nicer bric-a-brac when they're

Remodeling. (This monument itself
               Originally
Stood in quite another part of town.)
There he would sit, my younger self, enchanted
               Into furniture—
So full of himself, and just the verdigris
Of our old friend upon this pedestal
               Here in the park.

Tales of the Forebears

Her brother Paul had gone to prison.
There he learned to be a cook, and,
Rehabilitated, remained one
The rest of his life. Prison, however,
Diminished him, and I remember Paul
As a kind cretin with a plain wife.

His father played baseball. I do not,
Nor have I ever, been tempted to pretend
I like the sport. Such pride as there was
In that family extends to me from her,
My grandmother, whom I feared, despised,
And reverenced for sacred disabilities.

Martin, the only one of the four gene-bearers
I think if as possessing a Christian name
(For my other grandfather's *I* have inherited,
And the women were generically grandmas) —
Martin was a monster of obesity and complacent
Ill will. (He had been wounded in a war.)

Angels are both innocent and well-to-do.
My aunts Cecelia and Aurelia were in these regards
Angelic, descending on holidays to shower us
With gifts. I didn't love them even then,
So now I'm niggardly toward my own *nipoti*,
Who'll love me for myself or, likelier, not at all.

One house burned down; another was built of sod.
Both families officially believed in God.
The railroads killed some dozen Gilbertsons,
While tailoring warped my father's people's spines.
I am an atheist and needn't choose
Between a manly mangling and such servitude.

Working on a Tan

It takes work, he told me,
And you could see it did.
A tan so deep I thought at first,
Standing behind him, that his genes
Must have assisted. But no, as we shifted
Positions in the elevator, it was clear
He'd done it all himself. Incredible.
A compliment was called for, which
He accepted, like a diva, as his due.
And I wondered: *Could I, too?*

Now I'm equipped with a backyard,
Hammock, a stream with large flat
Boulders designed for basking—
All the right paraphernalia
For tanning. But I hide
Indoors with my typewriter,
Writing. The problem is
Without a lawn to mow, a patch
To sow and hoe, I am too much
A putterer to stay put.

To which the obvious solution
Has been to plant my desk out here
In the way of the sun and tan
As I finish the poem I've begun,
Its stanzas interleaved with pages
Of the ongoing novel. (I never could
Figure how anyone can justify poetry
As a full-time job. How do they get through
The day at MacDowell—filling out
Applications for the next free lunch?)

"Do I smell sour grapes?" jeers
My imaginary friend at the colony
(Whose every summer has been subsidized
For lo these many years). Her nose
Is accurate, and in this matter of a tan,
As well, it may be I am moved mainly
By envy of those whose copper tones
Betoken subsidies that need not be
Applied for—the social lions,
The skiers, the climbers, and wealth's other scions.

Who have, for all their patrimonial pelf,
Worked at their tans, while I myself
In mid-July am barely roseate.
Indeed, it is not, or it ought not be,
Their cash I covet but the care
They take to keep their carcasses
In good repair, their tans epiphenomenal
To the larger task of trimming
Sails and waists until fair Cythera,
And their abdominals, heave into view.

It can't be easy for that happy few
To leave off squeezing the wineskins
Of effortless pleasure and step into
The shoes of cowboys, farmhands,
Working stiffs. Once it was smart
To be palefaced and overfed. Now
Only hicks and mafiosi are complacently obese,
And so the bourgeoisie must work at seeming
As leisured as the class that can
Always find time for tennis and a tan.

It helps that Hollywood eroticizes
The clothing and complexions of the poor.
Without the lure of those confections
Who'd bother with cabanas at the shore?
Who'd buy the balms for quicker basting?
And what would these mosquitoes feed on,
If time and blood were not for wasting?
No doubt the race would keep on breeding,
If fashions in flesh tones were paler,
But I'd still burn to seem a sailor.

For say what you will, a suntan speaks
Of a purpose held steady for weeks and weeks.
Even lacking the *tout ensemble*
Of a body beautiful, at least being brown
Connotes an allegiance to something primal.
When skin and sun are one on one
And the sweat that tickled starts to stream
And consciousness becomes ice cream
That melts into dreams in your hand,
Then you're in sight of the land that's promised to the tanned.

Then the ultraviolet in the air
Reminds your melanin that *you are there*—
In Arcady beyond the reach
Of custom or of clothes, a peach
That's slowly burning into scarlet,
A fool, a simpleton, a common varlet
Asleep beside a golden veldt
Of Breughel wheat, feeling what he felt
Who first turned his face to the sun
And said, *Turn me over, this side's done.*

Swimming

As much as singing swimming
is essentially beyond
me. My torso doesn't turn
sideways in sync with my breath.
My vestigal legs in tow,
I paddle forward, slow

as a disabled steamboat, slow
as the clock on the swimming
pool wall. A will tow-
ing a whale. Ten laps and I'm beyond
caring what my laboring breath
sounds like. I take my turn

within the turn-
ing wheel of swimmers slow
as myself. I hoard a breath,
submerge, and splash my arms, swimming
towards that fabled flash beyond
conscious grasp, tow-

ards an order as tow-
eringly integral as Turn-
er's seas as they roll beyond
their blue horizons, slow
mastadons of color swimming
in their own deep breath.

The measured burning of the breath
as it fights the flesh's undertow,
the meshing of motions till swimming
becomes a single, smooth turn-
table revolving the vertebrae in slow
motion micro-ballets. Is that beyond

what I dare hope? And beyond
that, is there a higher order, a breath
so light, a light so slow
to dawn, a gift so reluctant to bestow
itself, I can't imagine it—and so return
to my original idea of swimming?

Swimming as hope, as a path beyond
past incapacities, as turn-on. Each breath
a lurch towards that goal. But oh how slow.

Entropic Villanelle

Things break down in different ways.
  The odds say croupiers will win.
We can't, for that, omit their praise.

I have had heartburn several days,
  And it's ten years since I've been thin.
Things break down in different ways.

Green is the lea and smooth as baize
  Where witless sheep crop jessamine
(We can't, for that, omit their praise),

And meanwhile melanomas graze
  Upon the meadows of the skin.
(Things break down in different ways.)

Though apples spoil, and meat decays,
  And teeth erode like aspirin,
We can't, for that, omit their praise.

The odds still favor croupiers,
  But give the wheel another spin.
Things break down in different ways:
We can't, for that, omit their praise.

March

The wonder of the high-flying kite
Resides in the string that tethers it
To your hand: it is a wedding ring
Unreeled to its full, true extent,
It is the laserbeam of love we feel
From the blue immanence above
Straight to the ache and pulse within
The skin's stout glove, it is this tingle,
This tug, this boing of telepathy
With the wind-frayed Olympian clouds,
It is the first hint we have of the size
Of the sky and our lives added up together.

A Cow of Our Time

AFTER CUYP

It's morning and the line has formed.
   I chew my cud and wait.
Sweet is the milk my blood has warmed,
    And kind is fate.

Still as I muse within my stall
   And yield to your machine
The paths beyond the barnyard call
    And fields are green.

Soon on that fragrant grass I'll browse,
   Beneath an elder tree,
And when I've had my fill I'll drowse
    Upon the lea.

From

The Right Way to
Figure Plumbing
(1972)

To Jean-Ann

There is no use
   falling in love
with the president of U.S. Rubber.
   Believe me.

If I were my own mother,
      or, rather,
      if you were my son,
I couldn't tell you any better.

For your own good, Jean-Ann,
      for your own
good, leave the president of U.
      S. Rubber alone.

The Blindman's Sign

I'm bitter and I wish
you bastards
were blind instead of me
I'd sprinkle salt into your bloody
sockets oh you would scream but as for me
I would drive
around the corner at 100 mph
I would describe the world to you
in painstaking colors
yellow and blue-pink and red and funny shades
of mauve
and I would kick
you when you weren't looking
more than once I would be *hideous*
if you could see me
you would be so terrified
that you would be glad you were blind

Thank you.

My Mother: A Discussion

Did I tell you about my mother? Yes
that is another myth we have here
She used to count
my toes my fingers and my toes
twenty of them altogether
so pink and tiny
and swab my ears
with oily Q-tips. She tickled me
Did she like to do such things? Who knows

Was it long ago? Yes quite long ago
No I forget I always called her "mother"
though she might have preferred
some other word
for all I know Sometimes I would meet her
accidentally on the street
Her or someone very like her A woman
at least. She was my "mother"

How did she dress? Yes
Yes very beautiful as I recall and pink
It all goes fuzzy when I try to think
My mother? True
I used to call her that
I used to call her my "mother"
but it is doubtful now
that such a person could ever really exist
Nevertheless it is a very famous myth

Everything Closes after Midnight:
A London Lament

I have turned into a pumpkin   I am poor
The ball is over and I did not dance
My heart stops beating   I am sad
Nothing can ever be so beautiful again
                              Nothing can

This is my usual corner   I'm at home
Here are the pots and spoons and darkness
I did not dance and now I am alone
My death drops down the chimney
                              My heart stops

Convalescing in London

Like a drunk treading on his trouser cuffs,
Time lurches past. Time goes too fast.
    I don't know what to do
And lie awake in the dark, overheated room,
    Listening, listening to
Time lurch past. Time goes too fast.

I may not move about too much, nor drink,
My doctors say. I went to the Tower today,
    Where many famous men
And women, waiting to die, found good things to say
    About death (a friend). Then
A few bridges and Hyde Park. Now it is dark.

Since my hepatitis I'm afraid
I've not been entertaining. It's too hot
    In here but when I raise
The window rain comes in, and noises
    From the street. I cannot
Concentrate on anything, except the clock, ticking.

"The Surprise"

My brain eats this gentle
music like a lentil
soup. I feed

& gasp
at the speed
with which the weeks sweep past.

I am sick
with idleness
& tell myself it cannot last.

Indeed,
it cannot.
I read & sleep & feed & play

the phonograph.
Now the music screeches
as it reaches

the scratch.
I bought
this record only yesterday.

The brain is made of just such wax,
& in time
it cracks.

Though I grasp
at straws,
Time will eat *me* when I am fat.

There is no refuge
from these laws,
there is no getting away from that.

Portrait of a Tourist

Here, my dear, my poor child—
this represents something good to eat,
and it's for you.

What will we do
here in Bolivia? What will we do?
But have you ever seen

such a lovely church,
Nora? No.
Now a woman dressed entirely in black

approaches us. The plaza
faints from the heat.
Thank you, thank you, but I really have more

than I can eat.
Don't be frightened by the blood.
Please don't be shy.

Pigeons light
upon the heaps of bodies in the fountain.
Have another bite

in this stanza.
Does it taste all right?
In America there is so much food!

But they must give us something
good, in return, these
Bolivians: they must love us.

Here, little beggar, please,
look this way—this represents me.
Give it a squeeze.

A Vacation on Earth

Chiefly, it is blue. People use
the old archaic words, which sound
larklike on their tongues,
not on mine. "I am fine,

thank you." Or: "Could you direct me
to the Mediterranean Sea?"
I ate an "ice cream" cone,
and I saw the recent Pope.

It is hard to believe
we have our source in this nightmare
tangle of vegetable matter and stone,
that this hell is where

it all began. Yet there is something
in the light or in the air . . .
I don't know what, but it is there.
I never thought I would descend

to such bathos! I did not come to Earth
to dredge up these worthless, weary myths.
There was no mother at my birth—
I do not need one now.

Yesterday I visited Italy: Rome,
Florence, Venice, and the famous church
museum. There was little I missed.
But tomorrow, thank god, I go home.

Learning to Cross the Street

How lovely the sidewalk is today
With all kinds of unusual bumps,
    Rounded and half-alive.
Soot-crystals melt in my eyes—
    I count to five.

Even the largest vans obey
The calibrations of the street,
    The arrows, stripes,
And blinking lights. White jet-trails
    Cross the sky.

Beneath the sheets of rock and concrete
Flow rivers of electricity
    And muck. White smoke
Slants into the skies of Battersea,
    And turbines roar.

I count to four, I look all ways.
It is not possible, from where I stand,
    To see the other side.
My fear is vast as cities,
    But I take your hand.

From

ABCDEFG HIJKLM
NPOQRST UVWXYZ

(1981)

Abecedary

A is an Apple, as everyone knows.
But B is a. . . . What do you suppose?
A Bible? A Barber? A Banquet? A Bank?
No, B is this Boat, the night that it sank.
C is its Captain, and D is its Dory,
While E—But first let me tell you a story.
There once was an Eagle exceedingly proud
Who thought it would fly, in the Form of a cloud—
Yes, E is for Eagle, and F is for Form,
And G is the Grass that got wet in a storm
When the cloud that the Eagle unwisely became
Sprinkled our hero and all of his fame
Over ten acres of upland plateau.
So much for that story. Now H. Do you know?
H is the Hay that was made from the Grass,
And I's the Idea of going to Mass,
Which is something that only a Catholic would do.
Jews go to Synagogue. J is a Jew.
K is for Kitchen as well as for Kiss,
While L is for all of the black Licorice
You can eat in an hour without feeling ill.
M is for Millipede, Millet, and Mill.
The first is an insect, the second a grain,
The third grinds the second: it's hard to explain
Such a process to children who never have seen it—
So let's go to the country right now! Yes, I mean it.
We're leaving already, and N is the Night
We race through to reach it, while P is the Plight
Of the people (Remember?) who sailed in that Boat
That is still, by a miracle, somehow afloat!
(Oh dear, I've just noticed I've overlooked O:
O's an Omission and really should go
In that hole—do you see it?—between N and P.
No? It's not there now? Dear O, pardon me.)

Q is the Question of how far away
A person can travel in one single day,
And whether it's worth it, or might it be better
To just stay at home and write someone a letter?
R's are Relations, a regular swarm.
Now get out of the car—we've arrived at their farm!
S is the Sight of a Thanksgiving feast,
And T is the Turkey, which must weigh at least
Thirty pounds. U is Utopia. V . . .
V simply Vanishes—where, we can't see—
While W Waves from its Westernmost isle
And X lies exhausted, attempting to smile.
There are no letters left now but Y and then Z.
Y is for You, dear, and Z is for me.

An Allegory

Three ballerinas in yellow chiffon
—these represent light—weave
their arms over and under, in and out,
clasp hands, then, rising
on point, clatter

across the stage: tacky-tacky-tacky-
tack. They seem to float. Wave
or particle? we ask ourselves, when
suddenly the theater
is plunged

in darkness, as some day zillions
of years hence our universe
will appear to fizzle out, much as if the same
three famous ballerinas
were to be seen

walking down a midtown street in rush hour,
too anxious or too old to interest
anyone. Then
the curtain call—
we all stand up and scream.

The Art of Dying

Mallarmé drowning
Chatterton coughing up his lungs
Auden frozen in a cottage
Byron expiring at Missolonghi
and Hart Crane visiting Missolonghi and dying there too

The little boot of Sylvia Plath wedged in its fatal stirrup
Tasso poisoned
Crabbe poisoned
T. S. Eliot raving for months in a Genoa hospital before he died
Pope disappearing like a barge into a twilight of drugs

The execution of Marianne Moore
Pablo Neruda spattered against the Mississippi
Hofmannsthal's electrocution
The quiet painless death of Robert Lowell
Alvarez bashing his bicycle into an oak

The Brownings lost at sea
The premature burial of Thomas Gray
The baffling murder of Stephen Vincent Benét
Stevenson dying of dysentery
and Catullus of a broken heart

At the Tomb of the Unknown President

Here the virgins he could not devour
In his lifetime are stacked like logs
In the great cellblocks of his friendship:
Each face wrapped in a famous silence,
Each leal heart a lamp whose flame consumes
The bonds of bankrupt cities. We have gathered
Here today only to stare at, and restate
Our faith in an innocence surpassing
Mere event, more real than measurement.
His madness makes us great, for who has not
Wandered, lost and exalted, in the forest
Of his lies? Who, witnessing his slow
Ineffable decline, has not tasted
The rarest vintage of articulate grief?
He has made the blind to see, the lame to leap.
For these and other reasons it is our belief
He is divine. Tears are therefore inappropriate:
We are persuaded that his corpse shall rise.

The Color Blue

We who are dead
Depend on the imagination.
Facts are useless, to us.
They are always the facts of life.

We believe all statements
To be equally true: that the sky
And its clouds are carved from stone,
That all words curve back
Into their roots,
That time is a tissue we unwrap
To find a ring, a scarf,
A miraculous kiss.

Always we revolve
A single endless thought
That is always new, that endures
Forever, that recurs
And recurs and is always new.

The Doppelgänger

Last night I dreamt I saw him in the park.
I stopped but he waited, patient as a lamp post,
In his flab and his pallor and his appalling clothes.
He's never threatening—only "interested." He wants to talk.
But I see the bulge his gun makes,
And I know some day he'll use it.

Meanwhile, except at the parties of friends we both dislike,
And in these dreams, I rarely see him.
His wife, who's the obvious original
Of the insipid women in his books,
Tries each time to bring us together.
"You have so much in common," she insists. And we cringe.

As to why or even whether I hate him I can't say.
Because he's my despair I'm unable to see him clearly.
And, naturally, I have no wish to.

D. W. Richmond Gives Directions to the Architect of His Tomb

As for the scenes at my office
I have nothing but praise for your work,
Just the amount of detail is extraordinary
& where your picture has departed from fact
I think I can see the reasons for what you've done.
However, I have two secretaries
& you have shown only one. Also, as I have pointed out,
I take frequent trips to Chicago,
staying there weeks at a time—& where
on the wall of this tomb is there any indication of that?

I have enjoyed your representation of my wife.
You manage to capture just those qualities
that make people love her. But somehow you miss
what it is that sets my son Richard apart.
At least you could show him carrying books, & in a darker suit.
My daughters, however, are excellent—so true to life!
But you must, beneath the figures, write their names:
Margaret is the one teasing a cat; while this is Laura
on the telephone; & the little one, Amy,
is alone in her bedroom, watching teevee.

As for this scene, where you have shown me at my pleasures—
this has been your masterpiece.
I have never seen such realism. Unfortunately,
however, I cannot allow these to remain here.
But if they could be detached—is this possible?—without
damaging the wall, I would pay whatever it would cost,
above and beyond that which has been agreed to already,
if you would re-install them in an apartment here in town.
I will furnish you with the address,
if you can accept so unofficial a commission.

Eternity

Yes I would love to enter immediately
into its annular enchantments to live
each never-ending moment without reference to
any other in a glow of pure Emersonian wonder
among those ever-trendy paradoxes that are not
exactly lies so long as we can feel them
ticking in our hearts like the mechanisms
of so many blissful unexploded bombs

And yet I really think that time is nothing
but a clock a simple arbitrary agreement to meet
together somewhere at a quarter after six
It is a precise quantity of very fine sand
a spring of known strength that is wound up and
winds down—It is the school where we pay
attention to the inexorable and are made to write
one hundred million times *I must learn to obey*

What is time—It is a trap we spring
with a single breath and in whose teeth we share
a common cruel fate with everybody everywhere
The difference is only that some are reduced
to elegy and others are able to chew off a leg
and hobble off to crystal shores and ruby regions
where the spray still lingers in the middle of the air
and time that used to bother us does not

There if we are absolutely still we'll hear
above the silence of the clocks a reassuring plash
as waters overflow the fountain's brim
in the courtyard of an ordinary mosque whose pavements now
do not disprove causality with rows of shoes
The doors are locked the worshippers dispersed
to wives and jobs—Eventually nobody believes
that noon is not the only reason for one o'clock

Homage to the Carracci

Limp as unwatered flowers, the gray limbs
And academic heads of vanquished caryatides
Droop from the illusory ledge, casting
Satisfying shadows on the ovolo, the astragal,
The egg-and-dart. This round tribune supports,
As well, a whole encyclopedia of engines
And machineries devised to pull down
The dome on top of us. Some of the pulleys
Already are in place, ropes taut, the frescoed
Laborers straining at the winches.
A crack's perceptible across
The cloud on which a god's superior anatomy
Reposes. He smiles, not oblivious
But as though from the first stroke
Of his natal brush he's been aware that
He, his pantheon, the cloud, the crack, and all this
Foreshortened, revolutionary crew were nothing
But paint and plaster, ingenious and untrue.
God of this ceiling, let us worship you!

How to Behave when Dead

A notorious tease, he may pretend
not to be aware of you.
                              Just wait.
He must speak first. Then
you may begin to praise him.

Remember:
sincerity and naturalness
count for more than wit.
His jokes may strike you as
abstruse.
            Only laugh if he does.

Gifts?
They say he's mad for art,
but whether in the melting
elegiac mode of, say, this
Vase of Poppies
or, turning the mirror
to his own face, a bronze skull
gorging on a snake —
that is a matter of taste.
In any case, the expense
is what he notices.

What to wear.
                Some authorities
still insist on black.
But really, in this modern age,
your best is all that is required.

May

Such beauty, you say
Let us stop & admire
A moment, a day
The fields & the fire

God the great spider
Has caught you again.

A Note to Romeo

Through all the rehearsals we dreamed
Of packed houses and raptured marquees
Gross with the winking letters of our
Lovely names. We imagined our wardrobes
Transmogrified by stardom, our smiles sincere,
Our whims notoriously gratified. We were wrong,
Of course, but through no fault of our own:
That play was a bomb. I'm glad to be back here
In the provinces, doing Juliet again.
You can't beat the eternal verities,
And as for this hamburger, darling—*Je l'aime!*

Questions Your Children Are Certain to Ask

Why is the sky gray? And how do we know
In the fall, when the nights begin to swell
With cold, where the sidewalks go?
Why is the world everywhere closed
In a smile? Why is my heart
Locked out of reach in my chest?
Which is best—the light, or the warmth,
Or the sight of the sun as it sinks in the west?
How do the different prohibitions grow
On fenceposts and the trunks of trees?
Are they alive? Are nails their roots?
How many moments make one slice of cake?
How many chairs are a life? If I swim
In the engines that power the lake, will I die?

The Rapist's Villanelle

She spent her money with such perfect style
The clerks would gasp at each new thing she'd choose.
I couldn't help myself: I had to smile

Or burst. Her slender purse was crocodile,
Her blouse was from Bendel's, as were her shoes.
She spent her money with such perfect style!

I loved her so! She shopped—and all the while
My soul that bustling image would perfuse.
I couldn't help myself: I had to smile

At her hand-knitted sweater from the Isle
Of Skye, at après-skis of bold chartreuse.
She spent her money with such perfect style.

Enchanted by her, mile on weary mile
I tracked my darling down the avenues.
I couldn't help myself. I had to smile.

At how she never once surmised my guile.
My heart was hers—I'd nothing else to lose.
She spent her money with such perfect style
I couldn't help myself. I had to smile.

Zewhyexary

Z is the Zenith from which we decline,
While Y is your Yelp as you're twisting your spine.
X is for Xmas; the alternative
Is an X-ray that gives you just one year to live.
So three cheers for Santa, and onward to W.
W's Worry, but don't let it trouble you:
W easily might have been Worse.
V, unavoidably, has to be Verse.
U is Uncertainty. T is a Trial
At which every objection is met with denial.
S is a Sentence of "Guilty as Charged."
R is a Russian whose nose is enlarged
By inveterate drinking, while Q is the Quiet
That falls on a neighborhood after a riot.
P is a Pauper with nary a hope
Of lining his pockets or learning to cope.
O is an Organ transplanted in vain,
While N is the Number of "Enemies Slain":
Three thousand three hundred and seventy-three.
If no one else wants it, could M be for Me?
No, M is reserved for a mad Millionaire,
And L is his Likewise, and goes to his heir.
K is a Kick in the seat of your pants,
And J is the Jury whose gross ignorance
Guaranteed the debacle referred to above.
I's the Inevitability of
Continued inflation and runaway crime,
So draw out your savings and have a good time.
H is your Heart at the moment it breaks,
And G is the Guile it initially takes
To pretend to believe that it someday will heal.

F is the strange Fascination we feel
For whatever's Evil—Yes, Evil is E—
And D is our Dread at the sight of a C,
Which is Corpse, as you've surely foreseen. B is Bone.
A could be anything. A is unknown.

From

Burn This

(1982)

High Purpose in Poetry: A Primer

for A. R. Ammons

Only one thing is needed: to speak of matters elemental.
Of sand and dust, in all their multifarious forms,
But especially as dunes (which are "mountains

Recollected in tranquillity"), of anything as basic
As water, fire, earth, or air: to lift it up and say of it.
There! Behold! to take the old hurly-burly of the world,
Its cyclones, coral reefs, tarns, and railroad tracks,

And fold them into a single affirmation, one massive Yes
Encompassing all facts, all laws, all sizes from the wee
But mighty force that knits electrons, quarks and positrons
Into a net of kinship more complex than that which unites
The most obsessed of aborigines, among whom

Marriage to a second cousin twice-removed
May be construed as incest, to the friendly and majestic force
Of the far-off sun, whose warmth and light and X-rays
Glide, noiseless, through the universe, observed

(If at all) by solemn spectrometers in institutes
On the planets of stars as beneficent (perhaps)
As ours (for our sun, you know, is only one

Of what may be a whole infinitude of stars!): a Yes,
Furthermore, to the entire range of beings in between
The subatomic and the astronomical: to, for example,
The elm trees of Minneapolis, dying of Dutch elm disease,

To the dear birds about to be evicted, to the worms
They would have eaten, and the lawns, mown and unmown,
Among whose roots those worms are ever on the move:
In fact, what is there one may *not* affirm
To mutual advantage? for in affirming anything

Do we not, in effect, declare our souls
To stand in some provable proportion to
The object of their affirmation? it is a kind of
Affiancing, if not a marriage quite, a promise

To the sturdy world that we will go on coexisting
On terms, which we have set forth, of love and trust, albeit
With an eye peeled for predators and natural catastrophes:

For it would be sheer folly to deny such things can be,
Though as long as they're kept at a reasonable distance
From one's desk they're harmless enough, and even
Instructive: indeed, they are affirmable as grass: so

Say Yes to the African lion, and Yes to the merciless
Typhoon, and Yes even to killers crazed with drugs
And to the businessmen who supply them with their necessities,
Trying, meanwhile, to stay out of their way: in general, however,
It's best for affirmation to be limited to those objects in

Nature that can't reply: for imagine if a murderer
Or even the loan application examiner at your local bank,
Finding himself affirmed, were to decide that your Yes
Was insincere or failed to do justice to his condition—

Did not, for instance, take into account the phlebitis
That was driving him nuts: then you might be
Killed, or at any rate your application for a loan

Might be turned down, and the improvements you had planned
Would not be possible for yet another year,
And then you'd have to praise a leaking roof
Or a 1962 Plymouth Belvedere that barely moves,

And all because you had, in effect, misdirected
A smile: too late then to deplore the world's
Inequity, or any single person's in it, for
Your affirmations were so broad that logically
You must appreciate all cases, instances, and facts

On the theory that whatever is, is right, including
Enemies of whatever dimensions, from viruses to
Supernovae: too late to say, "Yes, but . . ." if you want
To preserve so much as a scrap of consistency or

Self-respect: avoid, therefore, or leave to novelists,
All human specificities: if figures must be
Introduced into a landscape for purposes of scale

(And usually a cow will serve as well) make them such generic
Types that viewers of the canvas cannot fail
To see them simply as instances of an agreeable,
Fleshy warmth amid the coolness of so many greens (like sections

Of tomato on top of spinach leaves): speak of
Mothers and sons, of workers whose rough hands you can imagine
Shaking, of dreamy adolescents and their dreams, but do not
Mention anyone by name, or if you must, at least impute
To them actions of a character so neutral as to tend

To uphold a general drift westward to affirmation,
Where all the facts of life have gathered like a jury
Of sand dunes convoked on a cyclorama high,
High above the box where the defendant stands accused,

Whose answer to every question is and ever shall be Yes:
Yes, that was what I wanted: Yes, that is who I am:
Until both sky and dunes dissolve into one all-sufficing Yes!

For Marilyn Hacker

We are too fretful, you and I,
For our own good, or for our art's.

The heart is like a butterfly
That flits about in fits and starts.

The artist's task is patiently
To stalk it, catch it, classify.

He cannot take the time to ask
The butterfly about his task.

He craves its iridescent wings
Too much to mark its sufferings.

The heart surrenders him its facts
But never, hopelessly, affection,

And he must justify his acts
By the scope of his collection.

Praise

For you, Martti Talvela: your Boris is a bite of the original,
The wholly bitter heart of darkness, a Boris I could never have
Imagined myself, for my wits are too easily fuddled with
The pathos of Feodor, already a ghost in his own nursery.
Six months a year, I'm told, you work your farm in Finland,
Raise a large family, and run an opera festival. Who can refuse
Applause—if not for virtues only surmised then for
Performances unarguably fine? What else can be praised
But action sustained for no other apparent motive than
A developed sense of duty, friendships persisted in despite
The bad luck of a dozen sour conversations? (Yet what friend
Would I dare praise for that? It would be seen as just
A devious complaint.) So: I'll praise our mailman
For bringing our mail; I'll praise Leo Ecker, our super,
Who yesterday tried to repair a leaky faucet—not for free
And not successfully, but even so I think he's honest within
The sphere of temptations open to New York supers. He grew up
In Vienna and fought in World War One, and every year he can
He pays a visit back to the grave of his youth. Perhaps
That is what is most praiseworthy—to live
At an enormous distance from one's home. Once
On the train from Rome to Naples I met a priest
Who was returning to his village in the toe of Italy
After a stint of eight or nine years in Africa. He showed me
The souvenirs he was bringing to his relatives, a lot of gimcrack
Carvings of the kind you used to see so much of
In the fifties. One of them, an antelope, had had its horn
Snapped off inside the suitcase. The priest was close to tears.
To have reduced one's vanity to such an infinitesimal
Needle's eye. . . . Or is it rather that he preserved
A fragile virtue only to see it turn in the end to junk?
Whichever, my hat is off to him—and Gloria, to you,
Although we're not supposed to be on speaking terms. You try
So hard. How many sauerbratens have you made and never

Tasted? How many hundreds of stupid children taught to sing?
I am not relenting, mind you. Our merits can extenuate our faults
Only for so long. Then. . . . That's what tragedy is all about—
That we're condemned to turn away from those whom we accept
As equals, that no one can sustain the global weight
Of all that we require, that every decibel of our applause
Is a misrepresentation. Don't you always squirm
When the recording engineer leaves on those opening seconds
Of our roars? Isn't it better to sneak down the stairs
In silence? With the decent reticence of murderers,
Who leave no fingerprints, who leave without saying goodbye.

Poems

for Joyce Kilmer

I think that I shall never read
A tree of any shape or breed—
For all its xylem and its phloem—
As fascinating as a poem.
Trees must make themselves and so
They tend to seem a little slow
To those accustomed to the pace
Of poems that speed through time and space
As fast as thought. We shouldn't blame
The trees, of course: we'd be the same
If we had roots instead of brains.
While trees just grow, a poem explains,
By precept and example, how
Leaves develop on the bough
And new ideas in the mind.
A sensibility refined
By reading many poems will be
More able to admire a tree
Than lumberjacks and nesting birds
Who lack a poet's way with words
And tend to look at any tree
In terms of its utility.
And so before we give our praise
To pines and oaks and laurels and bays,
We ought to celebrate the poems
That made our human hearts their homes.

A Concise History of Music

When the wells of song were sweet
   In the childhood of the world
And tambourines jingled and bagpipes skirled
   And drums would beat with the beat
Of the heart, there was no art that hands and feet
   Didn't perfectly understand.
      And wasn't life grand?
      O, life was grand.

But the wells of song grew foul,
   And no one who heard them knew why
The hautboy would scream like a jet in the sky
   And viols would seem to howl
And the harpstring's sound was the cry of an owl.
   No, no one understood
      How songs so lovely could
      Cease to be good.

A Bookmark

Four years ago I started reading Proust.
Although I'm past the halfway point, I still
Have seven hundred pages of reduced
Type left before I reach the end. I will
Slog through. It can't get much more dull than what
Is happening now: he's buying crepe de chine
Wraps and a real, well-documented hat
For his imaginary Albertine.
Oh, what a slimy sort he must have been—
So weak, so sweetly poisonous, so fey!
Four years ago, by God!—and even then
How I was looking forward to the day
I would be able to forgive, at last,
And to forget *Remembrance of Things Past*.

From

Orders of the Retina

(1982)

The Goldberg Variations

When suddenly a tricycle got up
with Christmas bells started bouncing down
the stairs, and then with just a tremor
of hesitation (think of the too-strenuous
handshake of an aging banker) turned
round the corner, to encounter its own
image; so might a child in a hospital
bed, leafing through old magazines,
come upon a photo of his own face
in some ad for an obscure charity—
without astonishment, without feeling sad.

Litany

Sender of blue days & blissful silences
Sponsor of dreams
Theorem of a Grand Bahama
Thumbprint of the soul
Source of all stories & their final draft
Four-color separation of the unattainable Ideal
Idol before whom all idols else must bow
Fountain of the waterglass
Believer of all things unbelievable
Incredible giraffe
                    Misere nobis

Smiling pavement of a perfect street
Prince of lost shoes
Supreme graffito in the washroom of the world
Laughter of midnight telephones
Voice & velocity of light
Unwitnessable glade
Whiteness within the lie
Sweet beribboned lamb of stone
Alarmclock of eternity
Doctrine most dear
                    Ora pro nobis

The Childhood of Language

for Chip and Iva

The tree isn't here, and I am
Not asleep. Sometimes there are
Children in the tree. Sometimes
He takes me out into the other room
Before the grown-ups have left.
Sometimes he holds me up
And I can touch the ceiling.
Tomorrow when he takes me to the park
I will say the right word,
I will say "tree" and maybe he will untie
My shoes and let me walk upside-down
On the blue ceiling of the tree,
And all the grown-ups will have to watch
Me, the wonderful baby.

What It Was Like

Like a wine that burns the tongue
And leaves it thirstier, like glimpses
Into lit interiors from the windows
Of slow-moving trains, like rain
On pavements when the sky is clear,
Like isolated lines of verse
Reverberating in the mind,
Like figures in disturbing dreams
Condensed by waking to an article
Of clothes, like the loud cries
Of frogs or insects in the night
Or like the golden light of sundogs
Through a rift of cloud, like memories
Of wordless lies, like flies that buzz
About an opened fruit, like clothing
Folded in a drawer or like a pain
That vanishes as soon as felt,
Like butter melting in a bowl
Or like the color of a shoal of sand
As waves wash over it, like salamanders
Scurrying from walls, like postcards
Of suburban shopping malls,
Like scores of games with penciled names
Of friends forgotten long ago or like
A song dissolving in an empty room
While in the street below imported saplings
Glitter in the passing lights of cars.

Turner Jigsaw

The sea's complete, the sky is all to do—
Except the portion over to the right
Where sunlight pierces the clouds to pure flake white,
Transmutes a yielding oyster-grayness to
A faltering and then a limpid blue.
Now to sort out varieties of light:
Some featureless and some with malachite
Marblings; some bright, some dull; all but a few,
However, like as homonyms, of a hue
That can't be called gray and isn't quite
A blue. Since color offers so little clue,
It might make sense to go by shape. This bite
Must have a knob that it attaches to,
Which yearns, as stalagmite to stalactite,
Towards some other missing knob. I knew
I never should have started this. I'm through:
As much is done as I will ever do.
Back in the box! Good riddance and good night.

The Prisoners of War

Their language disappeared a year or so
after the landscape: so what can they do now
but point? At parts of bodies, at what
they want to eat, at instrument panels, at
new highways and other areas of intense
reconstruction, at our own children smiling
into cameras, at the lettering on cannisters,
at streaks of green and purple, at the moon,
at moments that may still suggest such concepts
as "Civilization" or "Justice" or "Terror,"
and at ourselves, those still alive, who stand
before what might have been, a year ago, a door.

Coming of Age

Here's the treason he didn't foresee:
Not a willing rush to the main advantage
The way that Jack instantly succumbed
To his wife's father's wherewithal;
Not even the grudging surrender
Of fresh tar to the feet of midtown pedestrians
As when Alice finally stopped trying
To dance; not the petulant despair
Of Max, stoking his emphysema
With forty Camels a day; nor Evan's defections
From the successive governments
Of his three wives—none of these.
Simply the depletion of reserves,
The discovery on the coldest night of the year
That there isn't any fuel for the furnace,
The disappearance of a smile still bright at 3 A.M.

What to Accept

The fact of mountains. The actuality
Of any stone—by kicking, if necessary.
The need to ignore stupid people,
While restraining one's natural impulse
To murder them. The change from your dollar,
Be it no more than a penny,
For without a pretense of universal penury
There can be no honor between rich and poor.
Love, unconditionally, or until proven false.
The inevitability of cancer and/or
Heart disease. The dialogue as written,
Once you've taken the role. Failure,
Gracefully. Any hospitality
You're willing to return. The air
Each city offers you to breathe.
The latest hit. Assistance.
All accidents. The end.

From

Here I Am,
There You Are,
Where Were We

(1984)

Here I Am

Coal Miners

From my vantage in the company's office
I never cease to admire our coal miners'
Philosophic composure before the problem
Of faith. In fact I was one of the first
On our floor to fight for the right to wear denim.
I know it fools no one, exerts no claim
And makes me look ridiculous in the eyes
Of Upper Management but how else, if I can't speak
To them directly, can I express my canine willingness
To let their Man be leader of the pack?
These small homages to the icons of his tragic vigor
Only allow us less guiltily to hypothesize his life
Underground: how he attacks the spangled earth,
Advancing slowly down its major arteries impelled
By an anger his own unholy din every moment renews.
His skin, like the limestone of a sea-worn cliff,
Has become one magnificent callus. His lungs
Are more dense with death than any cowboy's,
Whatever his cigarette. Because he has inhabited
Even this depth of darkness with the light
Of a common purpose his soul is socialized
To a degree we can but dimly imagine. Let us at least
Do that. Let us honor the dowdy churches
And ephemeral pornography that allow him to breed
Responsive sons who'll carry on the ruinous fight
With the first terrific lunges of a man's whole strength.
Let us wear, if only in our bedrooms or on certain
Holidays, a lantern on our heads in honor
Of his conquest of despair. Dare we suppose that ours
Is larger? But as for approaching him
In friendship, as for asking him to recognize
That by signing his paychecks in sanctioned simulation
Of the boss's signature we can be useful too—
No, that won't do. If they could hear us maundering

In the fictive caverns of our mirrored bars,
They'd only damn our condescending eyes.
Our kindnesses to them must be invisible or so discreet
As to seem so: building the movies that let them dream
Of houseboats, spies in helicopters, just desserts,
Of Samson as he detonates the jet-black pillars
Of one subterranean temple after another,
Then carts away their shattered Baals
To be burned in a million benevolent mills.
This much we'll do, and more: for ravaged skins
We'll sell a soap and call it ever-springing Hope.
On Saturdays, between advertisements for beer,
We'll share their ritual brutalities and cheer them on.
But we must not ask to be imagined in return.
Our business suits and busy minds, disabling fears
And air-conditioned air, cannot engender
Reciprocal myths. Perhaps it is Virgilian of me,
But I'd prefer my brothers underground
To believe in their inalienable rightness.
I'd rather they didn't know too much
Of the contents of my desk, the source
Of my pride, the force of my imagination
As it gnaws at the dark walls that surround me.

Prayer to Pleasure

Again! Oh glorious, I feel as though—Again
This wonderful sensation when I rub my hand
Against it: an effervescence of my very bones;
A bursting followed by a blessedness of peace,
Which I repeat at will. Tender oblivion!
Angel chorus! You ravishing, you glorious

Pleasure! Fill me past brimming with your glorious
Elixir! Excellent and only god, again
Destroy me with my wishes! Bring me oblivion
Perfect, eternal, entire! Come—give me your hand
Where jewels cluster like the scars of kisses! Peace
Be with you, and peace with me! Grind my bones

Into your bread, beloved! What use have I for bones
Or bread since I am blinded by your glorious
Periodicities? Before fermenting peace
Can turn to loss or need, I call to you again,
And you reply, my Pleasure, for ever at hand,
Never asking any price above that oblivion

I joy to spend my being in, the oblivion
Of delights endlessly reborn among the bones
Of sailors and their willing whores. Hand after hand
Was dealt them and they always played the glorious
Old game—eagerly too, the dears! Time and again
They won and lost and rest now not so much in peace

As in expectation of another piece
Of ass, another tug at the tits of oblivion.
When lunch is over, don't *we* hope to dine again?
And after dinner don't we save the chicken bones
For stock, thereby declaring faith in the glorious
Renewal of our appetites? To live from hand

To mouth—why not, since there's no other way? The hand
Is full, the mouth is satisfied, a perfect peace
Prevails. Ah Pleasure, it is you! Glorious
Provider! Sweet gushing source of my oblivion!
Drink up my marrow but return me to my bones
So that tomorrow you may suck them dry again!

Again I wait for you and place in your soft hand
These useless bones and scraps of meat, Prince of My Peace!
Bring them oblivion, Being most glorious!

Just before the Cops Arrive

Something terrible has happened
but I don't know what. The letter
that arrived this morning will say no more
than that another letter containing the bad news
is on its way. It is something so terrible,
apparently, it can't be named.
Humiliating too, I have no doubt.
Today is Saturday. There won't be
another delivery of mail
till Monday morning at eight o'clock.
For one weekend, then, I shall live
the life of an escaped convict, getting
steadily more drunk and more hilarious
as the dragnet closes in.
Sister Fidelis used to ask what we would do
if we knew the world was definitely
coming to an end in the next half-hour.
Hightailing it to church was not the right answer.
The thing to do, according to Sister Fidelis,
was to continue, unfluttered, at one's usual task.
Surely she was right. What better way to let God know
that one's conscience is clean? And mine—is it?
I believe so. Yet there is, for all that,
a sense of fitness to the nebulous but nevertheless
quite massive bad news, a feeling of
predestinate necessity that has less to do
with the symmetries of retribution
than with the fact that bad news is
ultimately inescapable. No matter

that we've reached another state, we're still
wanted men, on display at every jerkwater
post office. The letter may not arrive Monday.
A compassionate typist may have misaddressed it.
But even if I should never read it, even if
I should run away to Argentina, where they kill
anyone who prints bad news, it would still be there,
in its blue envelope, my own terrible truth.

Waking in a Strange Apartment

A table of walnut veneer, my second cup
of instant coffee, and three crinkly petunias
David picked in his brick garden to send over here.
I try to read my manual on motorcycle engines:
the clutch, when disengaged, allows
"an infinite degree of slip." Some people
understand the way things work; the rest of us
just float along and trust to luck
and the good faith of our repairmen.
Ed is getting up. Today he finds out
whether or not he has leukemia.

There You Are

Ode on the Source of the Clitumnus

There you are, waiting for me,
Or someone, to praise you. Propertius praised you,
Carducci praised you—it isn't enough.
    There you are, still bubbling away,
Filled with more fish than Nature unassisted
    Could possibly contrive, and not three yards
From the highway—in short, a perfect sight.
Walden Pond, which I have never visited,
    Is said to be in the same fix—clogged
With cans and candy wrappers, alive with the jokes
    Of tourists who drive there with no good
        Idea of who this Thoreau
Might have been or why he settled in of all place
    This, but who all certainly must have expected
        Something a little nicer.

But wasn't the world always a mess—especially
    Just off, like this, Via Flaminia?
        Without wanting to lay asphalt
On the last living blade of grass, one may suggest
    That any beauty, over-advertised,
Inevitably perishes. Mont Blanc has not survived
    Unscathed till now: then could
        The Source of the Clitumnus?
No. You will grow uglier year after year
    Until no one will stop to look at you,
No guidebook will mention your name, and poets
    Will have ceased to read
Propertius and Carducci; the Fiats and Peugeots
Will whiz by you in their haste to see St. Mark's
    Subsiding into the lagoon.

But still you will persist to rise
Miraculously from the earth, and while you do
You must be praised. Every day the world
    Grows poorer as the population
Soars. There doesn't seem to be much time
    Until the likeliest holocaust prevails.
        Billions of us, at least,
Will die, and this fact already begins to seem
A little tiresome. So we are dying—haven't others
    Died before? Yes—and that's exactly why
We must praise the Source of the Clitumnus.
    Not that you are beautiful, not at all—
        But because you have outlived
Temples, highways, and religions, and because
    You are there, waiting for us.

Ode on the Source of the Foux

The eye has reason to believe palm trees
   Superior to potatoes—but is it so?
   Is there more beauty in a chapel by Matisse
(I have not been to it, and do not mean to go)
     Than in some backstreet shrine
     Hallowed by a century
Of unassuming pain? Here in this once
Penurious hill town I find my own condition
     Writ large. I wince
   At the prices not so much because
I pay them but from the thought that I'm denied
     A share of the fleece.

   I hate the rich, and their police;
I hate the constant, conscious pressure they exert
     To keep me from their views—
     The seashores, mountaintops,
   And spiffy expanses that only money buys.
I long to live in a world I know cannot be mine,
     For they have it now
And mean to keep it as-is and all their own, selling off,
Dearly, only the cheaper bits: calves-foot, radishes,
   The thick mustard-color pots of Vence,
The unskilled smiles of waitresses too fat
     To earn better tips elsewhere.

     You say I'm cynical. Not so:
I live, like all of us, in the world I firmly
   Believe in, the only world there is.
     I wear the clothes I can afford
And entertain with a wine that mediates between
   Absolute pleasure and total despair.
   I share, like the rich I envy and resent,
     All priceless superfluities

Of light and air, patterns of sight and of sound;
    I offer words, and think it big of me,
        As gardeners take pride
In the jasmine they plant, the birds it fascinates.

Meanwhile, of course, the source of the Foux
Produces its usual profusions of the stuff
    Tongues and bellies most insistently
    Require—freely, one might think,
        If one didn't look too closely,
    If one didn't sometimes visit deserts
And inspect the bank accounts of their residents.
        Nothing is free, *mon cher,*
    Nothing—not the light, not the air,
        Nor yet, *ma foi,* these words:
They were learnt at the cost of as many years
As these hands have fingers, or these eyes tears.

    You blame me, and you always will,
For reckoning the cost and measuring the flow,
For hating what I hate and knowing what I know.
    I cannot help it, and I cannot stop.
        The fountain's water
        And the traffic cop
    Have issued from a single darkness
        We neither comprehend.
It isn't our enemy, but it is not a friend.
    I drink its water, admire the flow,
    But it's getting late, and we should go.

For a Derelict

Nothing matters. You are through
Pretending you're a grown-up.
From the wreck of your life
There is nothing to save.

The strain has been too much.
You are tired. You are very tired. So tired
You are nodding off
Right on the corner of 5th and whatever.

From between your legs
A sinuous stream of beer or piss
Follows the course of least resistance,
The course you follow too.

Not even the angels who gather
Over the doorway of Citibank
To bathe you in their tears—not even they
Can make you behave.

You are tired.
Nothing matters.
We cannot bear
To look at you.

You Can Own This Painting for $75

In the velvet shadow of an elephant
A clown is crying. Tears big as pearls
Drop to the page of the Dostoevsky novel
In his polka-dotted lap. His own child died
Of leukemia long, long ago. His wife became
A lesbian. His salary's inadequate,
All his experiences crushing. What living room
Anywhere could resist the icon of his smile?
Who, holding the fellow's skull to the light,
Would not wonder what thoughts once spilled
Through its sutures? Another glass of wine—
That's the only answer he will wink at now.
But listen: a trumpet! The elephant lurches.

Lost in the mists of her tutu, her torso
Wanders through terrible forests. Meanwhile
Her feet crush spring's first primroses,
Each step neat as a butterfly on a pin.
Now her hands are pinned to a windmill
And she is set spinning toward a new
Triumphant theorem: she falls, wounded,
Into its arms. Now the moonlight,
Like a fleet of cabs, circles the darkness
Where she hides. Throughout eternity
She will be thirteen years old: so
An evil magician has whispered to her shoes.
The poor pink ribbons glisten with terror.

Here is the world that never was
Where we grew up, and there's the sun
Licking the green lollipop of a tree.
The zoo peers out curiously from behind
Invisible bars. Seals honk and lift
Their primitive eyes to the blue paradise
Above. Keep us, they pray to the light source
There, out of harm's way, for we have always been
Good children. Their grandmother will vouch
For that, as she rocks all day in an armless chair,
Making change and longing for six o'clock
When her son will come and close her eyes.
She can remember every brick of her childhood.

When Your Hand Shakes, when Your Eye's Meat

When your hand shakes, when your eye's meat
In the lonely butcher shop of the mirror;
When every street's a corridor
In Home Town Jail; when you fail, and then
Fail again; when the lens of the door
Frames a stranger's weaselish face; when plot
Thickens and pace quickens and the
Graffiti won't wash off the wall;
When leaves sicken in the sun and records
Warp within their sleeves; when the weariness
Of many years claims another friend;
When pipes burst; when the first suspicion
Forms, when the hive swarms; when the poisons
Of the air plant their cancers in your flesh;
When no one answers, when the song exceeds
The breath; when the long-term trend of the market
Is down and stores are empty in the afternoon;
When you're transfixed within your room
By the squadcars' squalling rage;
When your hair goes, when your age shows,
When the cupboard's bare; when you walk
Along a graveled path alert
To the hungers of lovers and squirrels
And the world for a moment flutters
Its skirts and you're able to peer
Into the whirlpool of your fear.

When Your Eyes Meet, when Your Hand Shakes

When your eyes meet, when your hand shakes
The hand of the salesman who sold you the hat;
When you land on *Go to Jail*
And everybody laughs; when someone's
Radio is blasting along the street
But you can't resist the beat; when you're all
Clapping at the Judy Garland Revival,
Or when you join the singalong at church;
When you stop to watch and have to give
The obligatory quarter; when someone's daughter
Or cat crawls into your lap;
When you happen to meet a friend
And it ends in dinner, when someone says,
"You're getting thinner," and you know
You're not; when the store closes
And the happy clerks herd you into the elevator;
When the TV implores you to believe
In something other people believe in
And you do; when anything's exchanged;
When a strange restaurant lets you use
Its toilet free; when someone passes
In a style you completely agree with;
When a dog scratches a door, when the first guest
Rings; when people, in public,
Kiss, or fight, or conquer fear;
And when you're here, with me, at home.

Where Were We

A Catalogue

After the Tristan, walking past a row of posters
longer than all the Poussins in the Louvre,
or when you'd come behind me up a crevice in the rock
and the sheep I'd terrified jumped over your head;
Walking my father all over Tivoli, walking
in barley (as we afterward deduced) and being torn to bits,
walking to Marilyn's when she wasn't there, or, secretly,
to Chip's hotel; Walking to the Delaware,
walking to Rodmell, walking into Italy;
Climbing the vast garbage heaps on Monte Mario
the second day of our fast, walking through Ostia
with Berna Rauch, through Ely when your lens was killing you,
and in the twilight, through Chartres; Walking with our clothes off
but not very far, walking down literally
into a cloud, walking over Brooklyn Bridge, walking dazzled
by the boutiques in the Montreal subway;
Walking five days in the mountains with 50-pound packs
and never once escaping the hordes of other hikers, never once,
walking to where St. Francis lived inside a rock, walking
to Wordsworth's grave and the lovely teashop overlooking it;
Walking to Gloria's down Christopher Street,
walking on pavements that the leaves had turned
to glistening linoleum, walking in meadows
allegorical with cows, walking up various waterfalls;
Walking all over Paestum with a suitcase
and all over Pittsfield when its restaurants were closed,
walking home from *Buster Keaton Sulla Luna* and wondering
how it must feel to be world-famous and then no one at all;
Walking with groceries from Okewood Hill because they'd canceled
the Ockley bus, walking for miles in anoraks
until the rain had finally defeated us, then walking back;
Walking in the Tuilleries, walking on beaches,
walking in all seasons, weathers, and degrees of appetite
everywhere I've ever walked with you.

Alcohol Island: A Chronicle

THE JAWS OF SAFETY

Forget the past and make no plans.
While your seemly torso tans,
Plankton and planets swim and sink
And never feel the need to think.

Lift your eyes and still your hand.
Regard the sky, the sea, the sand.
When it is night the moon will map
Your way toward the waiting trap.

SERENADE

To be enclosed by green and living things
    Among the songs of birds;
To sleep and feel the while awakenings
    Beyond the reach of words;

    To cease from dusk to dawn
To need or think; to sink into the ground
    And lie within the lawn
And see the moon, from night to night, grow round.

SUN AND SEA

We went there for the season,
    And returned within a week,
There was no compelling reason—
    Just a general sense of pique.

It was hot—we knew it would be—
    And the beach was black with tar;
And we weren't all we should be
    At the fabled *Sol e Mar*.

The Clouds

Do you see yonder cloud that's almost in
Shape of a camel? *By the mass, and 'tis*
Like a camel, indeed. Methinks it is like
A weasel. *It is backed like a weasel.*
Or like a whale? *Very like a whale.*
Then I will come to my mother by and by.

Coral and shells are heaped until it seems
That everyone is rich, until the dreams
Of millionaires are clothing for the poor;
The world appears as it appeared before
The age of iron or the age of bronze:
Silvery beaches and wide, golden lawns.

Above all, changing: Perfect lambs one moment,
Moses the next, hurling his decalogues.
Elaborate as the handle of a silver spoon
Endlessly lifted to the perplexity
Of your smile. Smiling, collapsing—soundlessly
Offering themselves and moving off.

Slowly they graze the mountaintops, slow
Cows wandering home to their sunset—
Mildly anxious, leaking drops of milk
Into the monumental snow.
Now it is dark. Instead of bells, a blare
Of traffic and the chink of silverware.

A mother, fecund as Tuscany, pleased
To represent something so basically human
That even city people offer it
The yearly tribute of a Christmas card;
And yet she wonders who she'll want to be
Tomorrow when her babies disappear.

Love, you say—you love me. Then you become
A patch of sunlight propped against a wall,
A warmth that vanishes by three o'clock,
A pattern scratched upon a pretty stone,
A thought, a Romanesque basilica
With turgid fables flaking from the dome.

Or words—crisp unambiguous nouns, and verbs
Passing before us at an even pace,
Unswerving, with an army's iron grace;
But lovelier than these, if less distinct,
Those adjectives that decorate a blank,
White, wide, and slightly terrified face.

A wound, perhaps, but I've forgotten it
As if it were a dream that had recurred
Throughout my childhood: something orange, or red;
A flower, or a terrible mistake;
Someone at a previous address
Who gave me mittens, or who gave me socks.

An inclined plane, a wheel, a water glass—
Half engineering, half a work of art;
A human orrery that duplicates
The simple motions of the lungs and heart.
But turn it upside down and it becomes
Confetti circling in a paperweight.

As food flows into them, inaudible
To us, in cadenced shrills, they signal each
To each: I breathe, I move away, I need.
I need. The plankton, every molecule
Of water and of air is shaken by
The swelling and subsiding of their talk.

From century to century, the gist,
The motive antecedent to the act,
The indecipherable sense of it,
Even this, slips; the serried surfaces
Are left, draperies for archaeologists
To number and, provisionally, name.

You: you are the cloud I never name,
The language that I cannot learn, the game
I neither lose nor altogether win;
Illusion of another world above
The world beneath, outside the world within.
I squint, I blink—but still I see you, love.

Yes, Let's

Then let's have a nice time together, forgetting
our feelings of

let's let forgetfulness itself climb the staircase to
the unlocked delightful room where we invent our own
Saturday afternoon

because neither of us had the time to learn to sing
on key. The nun would prod each black notes with her long
wooden pointer and the class would quaver
along after

Yes, let's both ride our bicycles to the airport where
the wind has bashed whole trees down through the cyclone
fences and back into

feelings that were not at that time allowed
concrete expression

Tom Disch is the author of five short-story collections and eleven novels, including the computer-interactive novel *Amnesia*. He is theater critic for the *Nation* and a frequent contributor to the *New York Times* and *Times Literary Supplement*. This is his sixth book of poetry.